THEY'RE FAMOUSE . . .
THEY'RE FABUMOUSE . . .
AND THEY'RE HERE
TO SAVE THE DAY!
THEY'RE THE

HEROMICE

AND THESE ARE THEIR
ADVENTURES!

Great Job! Mrs. Moe

Geronimo Stilton

HEROMICE

FLOOD MISSION

Scholastic Inc.

The publisher does not have any control over and does not assume any responsibility for author or third-party websites or their content.

GERONIMO STILTON names, characters, and related indicia are copyright, trademark, and exclusive license of Atlantyca S.p.A. All rights reserved. The moral right of the author has been asserted. Based on an original idea by Elisabetta Dami. www.geronimostilton.com

Published by Scholastic Inc., 557 Broadway, New York, NY 10012. SCHOLASTIC and associated logos are trademarks and/or registered trademarks of Scholastic Inc.

Stilton is the name of a famous English cheese. It is a registered trademark of the Stilton Cheese Makers' Association. For more information, go to www.stiltoncheese.com.

ISBN 978-0-545-92010-0

Text by Geronimo Stilton
Original title *Missione speciale...diluvio universale!*
Original design of the Heromice world by Giuseppe Facciotto and Flavio Ferron
Cover by Giuseppe Facciotto (design) and Daniele Verzini (color)
Illustrations by Luca Usai (pencils), Valeria Cairoli (inks), and Daniele Verzini (color)
Graphics by Chiara Cebraro

Special thanks to Kathryn Cristaldi
Translated by Lidia Morson Tramontozzi
Interior design by Kevin Callahan / BNGO Books

10 9 8 7 6 5 4 3 2 1   15 16 17 18 19

Printed in the U.S.A   40

First printing 2015

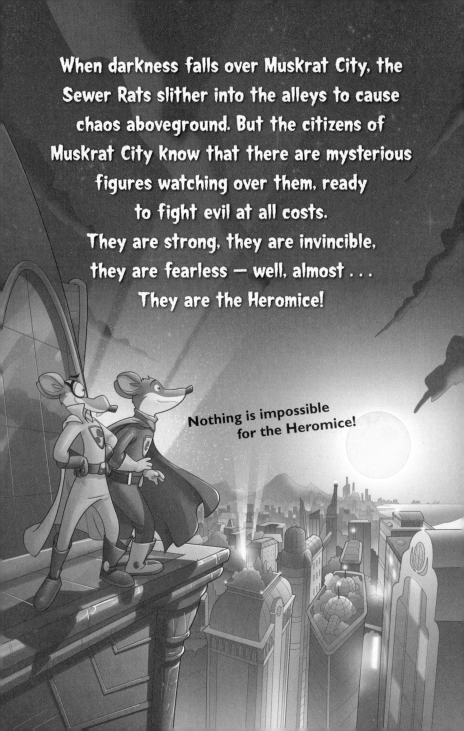

When darkness falls over Muskrat City, the Sewer Rats slither into the alleys to cause chaos aboveground. But the citizens of Muskrat City know that there are mysterious figures watching over them, ready to fight evil at all costs. They are strong, they are invincible, they are fearless — well, almost . . . They are the Heromice!

Nothing is impossible for the Heromice!

MEET THE HEROMICE!

GERONIMO SUPERSTILTON

The strongest hero in Muskrat City . . . but he still must learn how to control his powers!

SWIFTPAWS

Geronimo Superstilton's partner in crimefighting; he can transform his supersuit into anything.

LADY WONDERWHISKERS

A mysterious mouse with special powers; she always seems to be in the right place at the right time.

TESS TECHNOPAWS

A cook and scientist who assists the Heromice with every mission.

ELECTRON AND PROTON

Supersmart mouselets who help the Heromice; they create and operate sophisticated technological gadgets.

TONY SLUDGE

The undisputed leader of the Sewer Rats; known for being tough and mean.

AND THE SEWER RATS!

TERESA SLUDGE

Tony's wife; makes the important decisions for their family.

SLICKFUR

Sludge's right-hand mouse; the true (and only) brains behind the Sewer Rats.

ELENA SLUDGE

Tony and Teresa's teenage daughter; has a real weakness for rat metal music.

ONE, TWO, AND THREE

Bodyguards who act as Sludge's henchmice; they are big, buff, and brainless.

I'm Going on Vacation!

It was a **sweltering** Friday morning during a **sweltering** summer in New Mouse City, and I was, well, you guessed it, **sweltering**! Oh, sorry, I haven't introduced myself! My name is Stilton, *Geronimo Stilton*, and I'm the publisher of *The Rodent's Gazette*, the most *famouse* newspaper on Mouse Island.

Anyway, as I was saying, I was sweltering, but I was also excited. That's because I was about to escape the city and head off on a fabumouse **BEACH** vacation. I couldn't wait to relax!

I was going to a beach resort called **Whiskers by the Water** on

Cape Cheddar. I had even booked a class to learn **SQUEAKA SQUEAKA**, the latest dance craze. Normally, I'm really shy when it comes to **DANCING**, but

SQUEAKA SQUEAKA
THE LATEST DANCE CRAZE

SQUEAKA SQUEAKA looked like fun.

I was waiting to board the plane when my cell phone rang.

"HEEEELLLLLLOOOO, SUPERSTILTON!"

shrieked a familiar voice.

It was Hercule Poirat—er, I mean Swiftpaws.

"My name's not Superstilton!" I protested.

"It's Geronimo, and I'm about to leave on **vacation**!"

But Swiftpaws just snorted. "Listen, Superstilton, Muskrat City desperately needs your help. Now get your tail in **gear** and come on. Heromice in action!"

I groaned. Oh, why did Swiftpaws insist that I come on these Heromice missions? I'm afraid of flying. I'm afraid of criminals. And I always seem to forget how my superpowers work. No, I'm not cut out to be a **HEROMOUSE**.

"But my vacation . . . I mean, the plane . . . I mean, the *squeaka squeaka* . . ." I muttered.

As usual, my friend hardly listened to a single word I said. "No time for mindless BABBLING, Stilton! Grab your pen—the *Superpen*, that is—and hurry up. Last

time you were a little slow, remember?" he squeaked.

Rotten cheese rinds!

My relaxing beach vacation was *disappearing* before my eyes!

Still, I knew there was no reasoning

B-but my vacation!

with Swiftpaws once he had made up his mind.

"Okay, I'm coming," I squeaked.

I tried to find a quiet place to activate my *Superpen* and change into a Heromouse, but a LOUD whistle stopped me.

6 Tweeeeeeet! 9*

A traffic controller on the runway ran toward me.

"What are you doing?!" he shrieked. "The plane is **taking off**!"

I tried to explain that I had **changed** my mind about flying, but my words were DROWNED OUT by an enormouse plane headed right for me!

I turned as WHITE as a ball of

mozzarella! Rancid rat hairs! Squeaking in terror, I raced for the airport and slid through the doors just in time.

Phew! Safe by a whisker!

Suddenly, there was a **green** flash of light. Cheese and crackers! I was still holding my Superpen, and I had just pressed the *secret* button. I was turning into **SUPERSTILTON** right in the middle of the airport lounge!

At that moment, something began **M O V I N G** under my paws. I realized I had mistaken the baggage carousel for a bench! Suitcases, duffel bags, camping knapsacks, and what looked like two wrapped surfboards *SMASHED* into me.

OUCH!

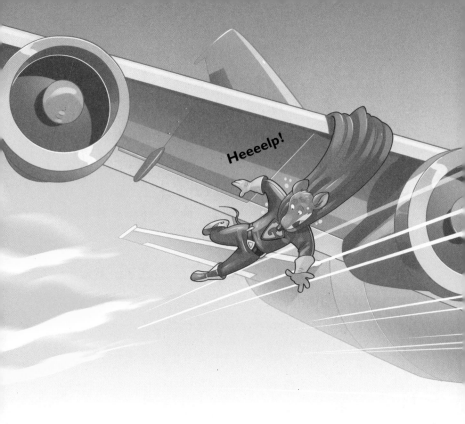

Luckily, my *Superpen* had done its job. Within seconds, I felt my paws **lift** from the ground. Before long, I was side by side with the same plane that had almost done me in earlier. From the window, I saw a little mouse waving at me happily.

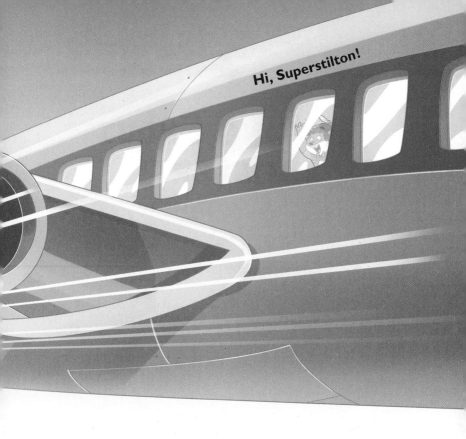

Hi, Superstilton!

I waved back, trying to look confident, like a real superhero. Then my cape caught on the wing, and I ended up hanging there like a *superfool*!

"Oh, I'm just really not cut out to be a **HEROMOUSE**!" I wailed.

Soaking Snout Whiskers!

After I untangled my cape, I headed straight for Muskrat City. The sun over the city was **burning**, and the wind was like a **blast** from a high-powered fur dryer. But when I veered toward the ground to land, I noticed that a tiny part of the city was covered with dark, billowing clouds. I heard thunder rumbling, and I saw lightning flash. I slipped inside one of the big clouds and . . . *WHOOSH!* A sudden downpour soaked me from snout to tail, and a bolt of lightning **SINGED** my whiskers!

My flight ended in a huge puddle of water! **Soaking** snout whiskers! How embarrassing!

Swiftpaws stood over me, shaking his head. "Do you really think this is a good time to PLAY in puddles, Superstilton?" he scolded.

I sat up and looked around. "How strange," I wondered aloud. "Why is it only **RAINING** in this part of the city?"

"Good question, Superstilton!" Swiftpaws agreed. "I'm sure it has something to do with those **nasty** Sewer Rats. They've plugged up the sewers, and all this rain has caused the Muskrat City River to **overflow**!"

The standing water had caused a huge **TRAFFIC JAM**, and a group of criminal Sewer Rats were robbing drivers. The Sewer Rats blasted the innocent mice with **HYPNOTIZING** sneeze zappers. Then, while the mice were busy **SNEEZING**, they handed over their wallets without realizing what they were doing!

"We've got to stop them!" Swiftpaws squeaked.

I followed behind on shaky paws. It wasn't that I didn't want to help. I was just **SCARED** out of my fur!

Then I spotted a big Sewer Rat zapping an unsuspecting rodent. Blistering blue cheese! I couldn't just stand there. I had to **HELP**!

"Stop right there, you, you . . . big, mean rodent!" I mumbled.

The rat turned around. "Huh?"

"Uh, I mean, h-how could you zap this **DEFENSELESS** rodent?" I stammered, trying to hide my shaking paws.

But instead of thanking me, the rodent put her paws on her hips and started **SQUEAKING**—at me!

"How **dare** you call me defenseless!" she shouted.

An instant later, she bonked me on the head with her purse.

Bonk!

"Did I say d-defenseless?" I stuttered. "I meant to say *delightful*." But the rodent wasn't buying it. She **WHACKED** me on the head with her purse again.

Whack!

Slimy Swiss rolls! Could things get any worse? They could.

After him!

Suddenly, four huge, **vicious-looking** Sewer Rats began to chase me.

Rats!

There he is!

I *scurried* on top of a car and tried to take flight, but something held me back.

"**STOP**, Supercoward!" yelled a Sewer Rat.

It was then that I realized what was holding me back. The Sewer Rat had grabbed me by the tail! The other rats were there in no

Huh?!

ZIP!

time. They tied me up like a supersausage.

"**HELP!**" I yelled. "Save me, Swiftpaws!"

But when I saw my friend, I gasped.

The Sewer Rats had **zipped** him up in a superstrong net.

"**MISSION ACCOMPLISHED!**" exclaimed the rats triumphantly.

I was about to start sobbing like a baby mouselet when a voice suddenly called out from nowhere:

"Hold it right there!"

When I turned, my jaw **HIT** the ground! It was the courageous Lady Wonderwhiskers!

WILD, WOBBLY WHEEL OF CHEESE!

Lady Wonderwhiskers stood on top of a car, GLARING at the Sewer Rats. Swiftpaws took advantage of the distraction to change himself into a pair of SUPERSCISSORS. Then he freed himself from the net. I wasn't quite as quick, and the Sewer Rats swung me by my tail into the air.

"Wild, wobbly wheel of cheese!" I shrieked, panicking.

But as soon as I said those words, a miracle happened. My cheesy superpowers activated!

Right then an ENORMOUSE wheel of cheese appeared on the sidewalk! It rolled toward the Sewer Rats,

knocking them down like bowling pins.

"Your powers are amazing, Superstilton!" exclaimed Lady Wonderwhiskers.

SUPERPOWER:
ROLLING WHEEL OF
PARMESAN CHEESE
ACTIVATED WITH THE CRY:
"WILD, WOBBLY
WHEEL OF CHEESE!"

Ouch, ouch, ouch!

Yikes!

"Um, right, my powers," I mumbled. I always seemed to **forget** how my superpowers worked. **OH, HOW EMBARRASSING!**

The Heromouse untied me as I stared into her kind and **sparkling** blue eyes.

"Thanks, Wonder Lady ... I mean, Lady Whiskers ... I mean, Lady **Wonderful** ..." I stammered. **OH, HOW EMBARRASSING!**

A voice interrupted me. "This time you got away!" it warned. "But your luck won't last forever, Supermeddlers!" It was the evil thug **SLICKFUR**!

Beside Slickfur stood **Tony Sludge**, the undisputed leader of the Sewer Rats and the number one enemy of the Heromice. Immediately, my paws began to tremble.

Then I noticed a young female rodent with **purple** hair and an evil expression.

Something told me she wasn't there to sell us a box of Mouse Scout cookies.

File No. 24127
Elena Sludge

Who: Tony Sludge's spoiled rotten daughter

Where she lives: Rottington

Passions: Botanical chemistry and innovative technology

Favorite music: Rat metal music

Hobby: Collects rare meat-eating plants

"Who's she?" I asked with a shaky voice.

"It's **ELENA SLUDGE**, Tony Sludge's daughter," replied Swiftpaws.

At that moment, Elena and Slickfur held up what looked like two small inside-out **UMBRELLAS**.

"Oooh! We're so scared! Tiny umbrellas!" mocked Swiftpaws. "Give it up, Sewer Rats. You're no match for us Heromice!"

"Hmmm . . . are you sure about that?" Elena snapped with a smirk.

The two rats pointed their umbrellas at the sky. Immediately, a bluish flash of light shot out from each umbrella. An instant later, a TORRENTIAL downpour descended on us. Super Swiss slices!

The weirdest thing was that the water seemed to be concentrated just on us! We tried to take shelter under our supercapes, but the downpour was too heavy. It felt like we were being SQUASHED by a solid wall of water!

Headlines flashed before my eyes: *Heromice Held Hostage by Deadly Downpour! Superstilton Gets Supersoaked!*

"Take that as a WARNING, Superpests!" Slickfur screeched. "You'll be hearing from our boss!"

As soon as the Sewer Rats left, the RAIN stopped completely! The clouds

Rain-triggering umbrellas

Take that!

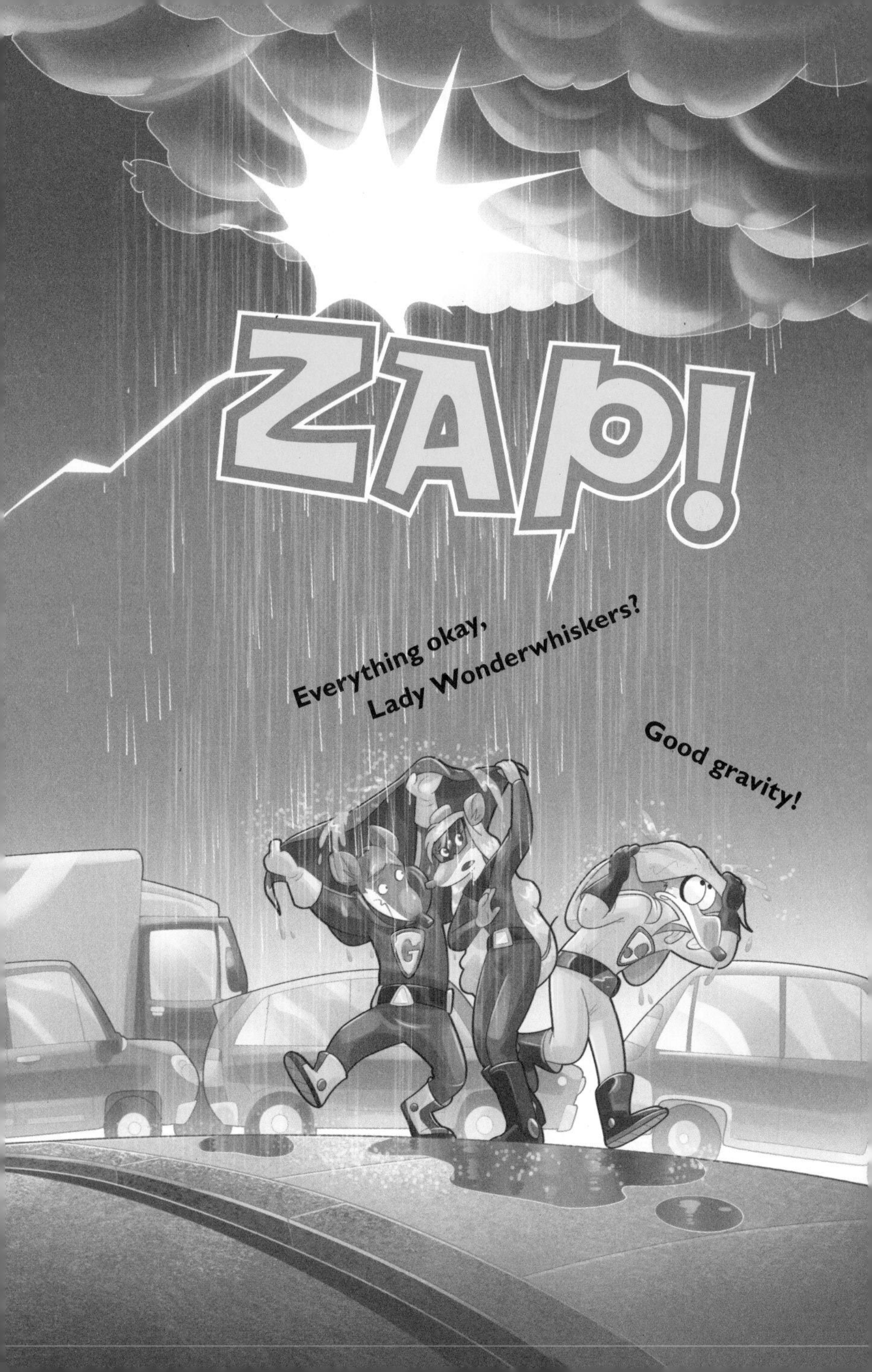
ZAP!
Everything okay, Lady Wonderwhiskers?
Good gravity!

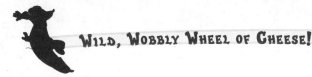

disappeared, and the sun came out. Talk about a sudden change in the weather!

How could two TiNY inside-out umbrellas cause such a disturbance?

SNOW IN THE SUMMER?

We headed straight to **HEROMICE HEADQUARTERS** to find out. When we arrived, our Heromouse helper, Tess Technopaws, and her friends Electron and Proton greeted us. I sank into a **comfy** pawchair in front of a fan and sipped a **refreshing** mozzarella milkshake.

I was just starting to **relax** when Muskrat City's police

Ahh . . .

commissioner Rex Ratford's **worried** snout appeared on the computer monitor in the control room.

"Heromice, is it true that Slickfur and Elena Sludge are wreaking havoc with the **weather**?" he squeaked.

The Sewers Rats are controlling the rain!

"It's true," answered Tess Technopaws, the head scientist (and also the cook) at **HEROMICE HEADQUARTERS**. "We suspect that the Sewer Rats have INVENTED a machine that can modify the behavior of the clouds."

"The Heromice have described objects that look like inside-out umbrellas," added Electron. "They're probably antennae that the Sewer Rats use to make *RAIN*."

Proton blinked. "Wait a second," he squeaked. "Before a system like that can work, the clouds have to be sprinkled with ice particles."

Proton was interrupted by a loud buzzing noise.

ZZZZZZ!

Was it a chain saw? Or maybe a swarm of killer bees?

Yawn . . .

No, it was Swiftpaws. He had fallen asleep, and he was **snoring** loudly!

"Do you mind?" Proton snapped.

"Sorry," my hero partner yawned. "All this science talk is making me sleepy."

With a **HUFF**, Proton went on to explain that the particles could be activated through a remote control.

"So the ice particles could be used to make rain, **wind**, or even snow!" added Electron.

"Exactly!" Proton agreed. "And I bet that **ELENA SLUDGE** is the one behind those ice particles. She's a genius in chemistry."

Right then, the commissioner let out a squeak. "Look!"

He pointed to the window behind him, ANGLING his webcam toward it. The landscape had begun to turn white.

"Snow in the summer! I don't **BELIEVE** it!" Ratford exclaimed.

A second later, the screen went BLANK. A sinister **voice** croaked from the computer's speakers: "Good afternoon, Hopelessmice! How do you like our little **snow** show? Heh, heh, heh!"

Am I Right or Am I Right?

Tony Sludge's ROTTEN face appeared on the screen. His daughter, Elena, was right next to him.

"Our SNOWSTORM is totally impressive," the evil Sewer Rat cackled. "Am I right or am I right? But we have something even more damaging coming to Muskrat City. Unless you meet our demands, a *flood* like you've never seen is headed your way!"

"D-d-d-demands?" I managed to stutter. "And what would those demands b-b-be?"

"Oh, nothing much," Tony replied as he unfurled a sheet that was a mile long. Well, okay, it really wasn't a mile long, but

you get the idea. It was *bong*!

Then he began to read: "A lifetime supply of cheddar cheese (but not extra sharp—it bothers my stomach); **five** mansions with indoor pools, hot tubs, and tennis courts; season tickets to the Muskrat Giants . . ."

TONY SLUDGE'S LIST OF DEMANDS

Listen closely!

An hour later, Tony was still listing his demands. "A two-hundred-fifty-foot yacht; a Mouserati **turbo** convertible; round-trip airfare to the *Cheesequake Islands* (Mrs. Sludge has been complaining that we never go on vacation); all the *jewels* and precious gems in the entire city; free membership to the WEALTHY WHISKERS Golf and Swim Club . . ."

Tony's voice **droned** on. Holey Swiss, would he ever stop squeaking?!

Finally, I couldn't take it anymore.

"But we can't possibly meet those demands," I blurted out. "Plus, they're a little silly."

Tony's face grew **red** with rage. "**Silly?!**" he shrieked. "I'll tell you what's silly—you and your **supersenseless** pals! You have two hours before you end up **underwater**!"

Elena pointed her weird umbrella contraption toward the sky. The snow stopped falling as suddenly as it had begun. Tony's and Elena's faces **disappeared** from the screen and were replaced by Commissioner Ratford's unhappy snout.

Are you ready for a flood?

"Heromice, we must *stop* them!" he squeaked.

SUPER-RAFTS

After Ratford hung up, Swiftpaws began SQUEAKING.

"Okay, mice, we have to put our heads together," he said. "But first, I know **exactly** what we need!"

He headed for the kitchen and made two **ENORMOUSE** sandwiches. And when I say enormouse, I mean they were **mammoth**, colossal, no, **GIGANTIC**! They were filled with everything you could think of: cheese, pickles, mustard, sauerkraut, olives, radishes, peanut butter, raisins . . . the list was **LONG**!

"Let's see now . . . *chomp*!" Swiftpaws mumbled. "First of all, we have to . . .

crunch! Yes, of course, and then . . . **MUNCH, MUNCH, MUNCH**. Not to mention . . . **gulp**!"

"Huh? Can you repeat that?" asked Electron. "We can't understand a word you're saying."

Right then my stomach let out a **GROWL** so loud I began running for the door before I realized I was **running** from myself. Oh, how humiliating!

"Here, try this," Swiftpaws said, offering me the other **SANDWICH**.

What could I do? I was **starving**, so I

> **SUPERSTUFFED MEGA SANDWICH**

1. Yum!

2. Uh-oh . . .

3. It's so hoooot!

grabbed the superstuffed mega sandwich and without thinking took one giant bite. Chomp! That's when I realized I had just made one **GIANT** mistake! Immediately, my eyes began to tear, smoke poured out of my ears, and my mouth felt like it was on fire! Oh, why hadn't Swiftpaws told me there were HOT PEPPERS in the sandwich?!

"Really, Superstilton?" Swiftpaws scoffed. "We don't have time for your dramatics.

The Sewer Rats mean

business! Now, as I was saying, it seems those rats used **SMALL** antennae to set off the rain in small portions of the city. But to **FLOOD** the whole place they would need hundreds of antennae."

You're a genius, Superstilton!

"Or they could use one really **GIANT** antenna," I mumbled, my mouth still **SCORCHED** from the sandwich.

"*Super Swiss slices!*" cried Tess excitedly. "That's it! You're a **GENIUS**, Superstilton! Now we just have to find that antenna!"

"So what do we do now?" asked Swiftpaws.

"Well, if the Sewer Rats

need to activate the clouds by **sprinkling** them with ice particles, why don't you Heromice fly **UP** there and check things out?" Electron suggested.

Instantly, my heart began **hammering** under my fur. Did I mention I'm afraid of heights? "Do you think that's really necessary?" I muttered as Swiftpaws began **DRAGGING** me to the terrace.

"Don't be ridiculous, Superstilton!" Swiftpaws shouted confidently. "**WE'RE HEROMICE!**"

"But I'm not cut out to be a Heromouse!" I cried.

As usual, my hero partner just ignored me.

Before we left, Tess handed me what looked like two **TINY** pieces of chewing gum.

"Take these," she insisted. "They may **save** your life!"

I seriously doubted that **CHEWING GUM** would save my life, but I didn't want to be **rude**.

"Thanks for the gum," I said as I took the pieces in my paw.

"That's not gum, Superstilton," Tess said with a laugh.

"Those are INFLATABLE rafts. In an **emergency**, place them in water, and they will expand to normal size."

Great **intergalactic** gadgets! What a fabumouse invention! I put the rafts into the belt of my supercostume and hoped I would remember I had them.

"Time to **HIT** the sky!" Swiftpaws shouted. Then, before I could stop him, he *pulled* me up into the clouds.

"HEROMICE IN ACTION!"

he squeaked.

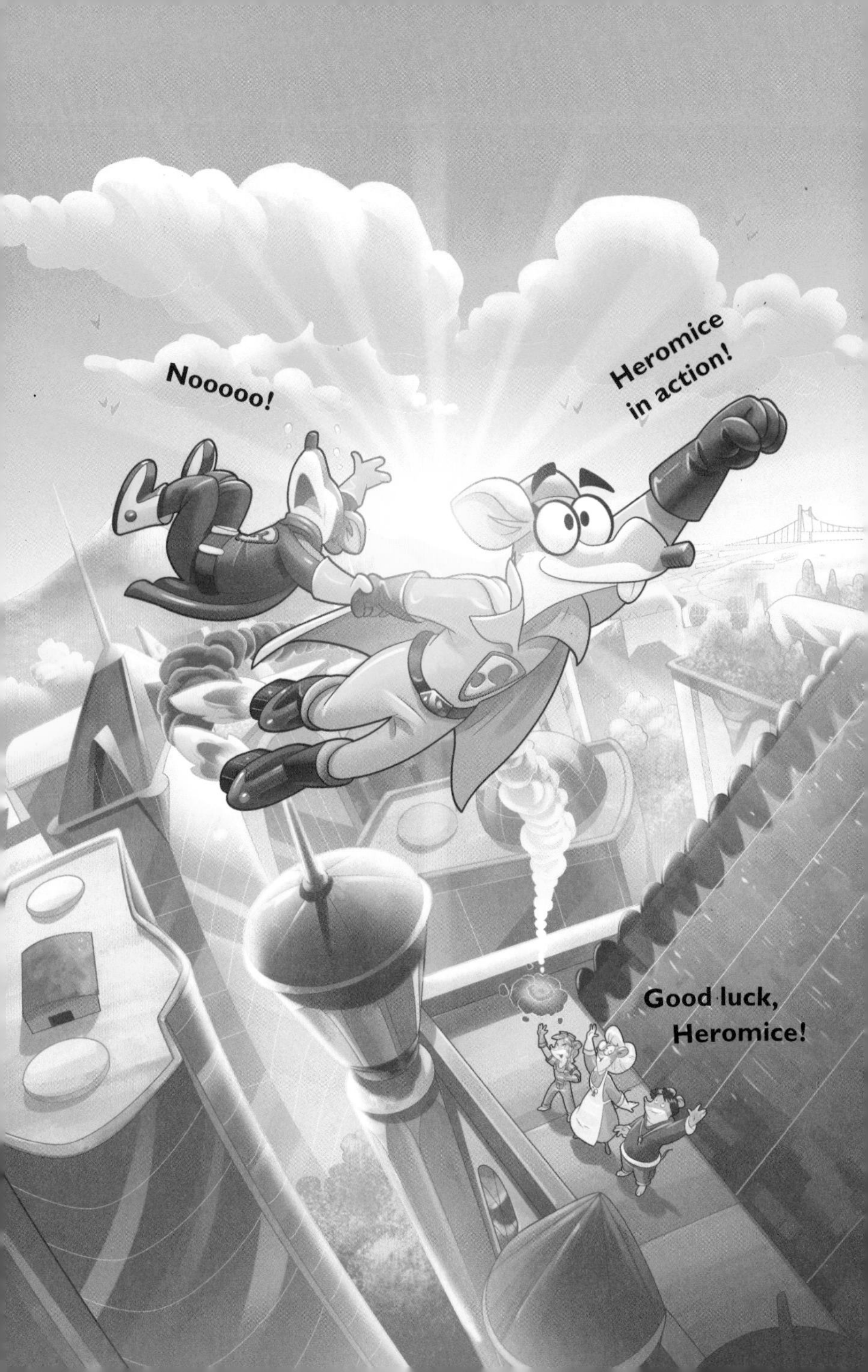
Nooooo!
Heromice
in action!
Good luck,
Heromice!

Don't Look Down!

When Swiftpaws let go of my paw, I realized I was flying directly over Muskrat City's roofs. **SIZZLING** solar panels! I was so **scared**, I had to force myself not to faint from fear!

"**Don't look down! Don't look down!**" I coached myself, taking long, **DEEP** breaths.

Eventually, I started to calm down. Yes, I was feeling better, **stronger**, and more confident . . .

Suddenly, Swiftpaws did a series of acrobatic moves.

"Hey, Superstilton!" he squeaked. "Look at me!"

He *TUMBLED*, *ZIGZAGGED*, and

BONK!

dove through the clouds.

I was so busy watching Swiftpaws, I didn't notice the *huge* flock of birds heading straight for us! Good gravity!

Before I could change directions, I crashed into the first bird . . . **bONK!** Then I collided with the second bird . . . **CLONK!** Finally, I bounced off a third bird, who let out an ear-piercing honk, honk!

CLONK!

HONK! HONK!

I ended up **BRUISED** and covered with feathers from my whiskers to my tail!

"Do you really think this is a good time to be playing games with a flock of birds, Superstilton?" Swiftpaws scolded. Then he held up a paw. "Hey! Did you hear that noise?"

My ears pricked up. At first I didn't hear a thing. But then I suddenly heard a whirring that grew louder and louder.

WHIRRRRRRR!
WHIRRRRR!

A helicopter appeared out of nowhere from behind a FLUFFY cloud. The pilot was a rat who looked very, very **familiar**. "*RAT-MUNCHING* space monsters!

That's **One**, Tony Smudge's henchmouse!"
I exclaimed. "What's he doing up here?"

A stream of thousands and thousands
of **SHINY** particles stretched behind the
helicopter.

"He's carrying the *little frozen*
particles Proton told us about!" exclaimed
Swiftpaws. "Looks like One is preparing the

clouds for an **ENORMOUSE** storm!"

In the meantime, that **ROTTEN** Sewer Rat was heading straight for us.

"Look out!" shouted Swiftpaws, dragging me with him.

"Your days are numbered, Hopelessmice!" snickered **One** as he aimed the propeller at my tail.

HeLP! I love my tail!

The Sewer Rat chased us around and around. Then, to confuse him, we dived inside a cloud. But we couldn't see a thing!

"Swiftpaws, where are you?" I shrieked.

"**Over here!**" he answered. "We've got to find a way out of here. Let's put our heads TOGETHER and think."

But we couldn't figure out what to do.

Finally, I decided I had to take *action*. So I gathered all my strength and began flying at *supersonic* speed until . . .

CLONK!

I crashed right into my
Heromouse partner! I guess
Swiftpaws had come up
with the same idea.
Talk about putting
our heads together!
OUCH!

Ouchie!

Now my head was **THROBBING**, and to make matters worse, the helicopter had entered the cloud and was hovering right next to us!

"There's nowhere to *hide*, Superpests!" One squeaked from the copter.

UH-OH. We were in big trouble.

1 Was Really, Really Dizzy!

The slimy Sewer Rat flipped his helicopter around in a BLUR of acrobatic moves. Then he shot toward us, nicking the fur off my tail.

"**Super-ouchie!**" I squeaked.

Swiftpaws took advantage of that moment to grab on to the helicopter's landing gear.

"Say good-bye, Sewer Fur!" my hero partner squeaked as he tried to climb into the cockpit. But a second later, One pressed a button, and a stream of smoke shot out of the helicopter, **engulfing** Swiftpaws.

Cough, cough, cough!

Cough, cough, cough!

"HeLP!" Swiftpaws squeaked.

Covered with black soot and **DIZZY** from the fumes, Swiftpaws let go of the landing gear and plunged toward the ground.

"Happy landing, **SUPERNUISANCE**!" sneered One.

Super Swiss slices! Swiftpaws was **spiraling** out of control.

"Use your supersuit!" I **SHRIEKED** to my hero partner. But he didn't hear me.

Rats! I had to do something quickly! But what? I was alone in the clouds, and when I looked down, my whiskers **trembled**

with fear. On the other paw, I couldn't let my friend **splatter** on the ground like a **four-cheese omelet**! So I took a deep breath, closed my eyes, and launched myself toward Swiftpaws. Every so often, I opened my eyes for a second to see where I was.

First I was fifty feet from Swiftpaws.

GULP!

I was *dizzy*!

Then I was twenty feet from Swiftpaws.

GULP!

I was **really dizzy**!

Finally, I was only ten feet away.

GULP!

I was **really, really dizzy**! Plus, I realized that I'd never reach my friend in time!

"Soaring Swiss cheese tower!"

SUPERPOWER:
FABUMOUSE
CHEESE TOWER
**ACTIVATED WITH
THE CRY:**
"SOARING SWISS
CHEESE TOWER!"

I shouted out in frustration. Oh, what could I do?

Then, to my surprise, my **SUPER-CHEESY** superpowers activated. **GIANT** wheels of Swiss cheese sprang from the ground!

The wheels quickly piled up one on top of the other, forming a very TALL and delicious-smelling tower. A second later, Swiftpaws landed on the **FABUMOUSE** cheese tower, sinking into it with a loud SPLUUUUFFF!

"Swiftpaws?!" I called. "Is everything okay?"

But all I heard from inside the tower was chomp, chomp, chomp!

I decided to climb the tower to see what was going on. When I got to the top, I called down, "Swiftpaws, are you alive?"

"Of course I'm alive," he squeaked back from inside. "Come on in, Superstilton! These Swiss wheels are AWESOME—

chomp, chomp, burp!"

Suddenly, my hero watch BUZZED, connecting me to Heromice Headquarters.

"Good news, Heromice!" exclaimed Proton. "I figured out which ANTENNA the Sewer Rats plan to use. Come on back!"

We got it, Heromice!

HERO WATCH CONNECTED TO HEROMICE HEADQUARTERS

My whiskers drooped. So much for tasting my fabumouse Swiss cheese tower!

Boing! Boing! Boing!

I told Swiftpaws the news, and he emerged from the tower still chewing. I stared wistfully at the *fragrant* wheels of Swiss. Ah, what a delicious smell!

"Superstilton? Are you still there?" Proton's voice SQUEAKED from my hero watch.

"Ahem, sure. I was just smelling the tower . . . I mean, the cheese . . . I mean, the air . . ." I babbled.

"The Sewer Rats are tampering with the ***Muskrat TV*** building's antenna," Proton said.

"Let's go!" answered Swiftpaws.

The ***Muskrat TV*** building was

in the middle of Muskrat City. It was a tall skyscraper packed with antennae and **HUGE** satellite dishes on the roof. When we got there, we found **Lady Wonderwhiskers** standing in front of the locked front doors.

"How do we get in?" she asked.

Swiftpaws stepped forward, PUFFING up his fur.

"Oh, Lady Wonderwhiskers, please allow me!" he said with a confident smile. "We don't need to go through the front door. I'll just fly straight up to the roof!"

Then he flew upward, spinning and tumbling through the air, showing off his most impressive flying moves.

"Wow! Look at him go!" Lady Wonderwhiskers squeaked, admiring my partner. Her BLUE eyes flashed with excitement.

"Er, right," I answered with a touch of envy. "He's not bad if you like all those flying tricks and —"

Suddenly, I was interrupted by a loud noise.

BOING!

When I looked up, I realized my hero partner had just *crashed* into something. But there was **NOTHING** there!

Swiftpaws tried again and again to get near the antennae on top of the building. But every time he tried, he bounced backward in the air.

BOING!

BOING!

It was as if the roof was protected by an invisible force field!

BOING!

BOING!

BOING!

Finally, he dropped back to the ground, EXHAUSTED.

"Okay, Superstilton, time for Plan B!" he squeaked.

"Plan B?" I spluttered.

What's . . .

Ugh!

. . . happening?!

Swiftpaws snorted. "Of course! Plan B is the backup plan. All Heromice have a Plan B! So what is it, Superstilton?"

Good gravity! I didn't have a Plan B! But everyone was staring at me. I cleared my throat.

"Um, er . . . well, you could change yourself into a SuPeRKey and open the front door."

"AWESOME idea!" cheered Lady Wonderwhiskers. Then she planted a little kiss on my cheek. I turned as red as a tomato.

My Heromouse partner didn't lose any time. Using his superpowers, he quickly

Awesome idea!

changed himself into a yellow key and tried to get in, but it didn't work. So he tried turning into a crowbar, a chisel, a jackhammer, a **WRECKING BALL**, and a steamroller. But nothing worked.

Finally, Proton's voice squeaked from our hero watches.

"Heromice!" he said. "I know how to get you in!"

I'VE GOT THIS!

Proton explained that there was a ventilation duct located at the rear of the **Muskrat TV** building. Now all we had to do was find it. We would be able to crawl through it into the building!

"We're ready!" Swiftpaws cried.

"Hurry!" Electron told us. "The Sewer Rats' **ultimatum** expires in half an hour!"

Ticking cheese bombs! There wasn't a moment to lose! But when we reached the duct, there was a huge fan blocking it.

I climbed onto Swiftpaws's shoulders and PULLED with all my might.

"I've got this!" I grunted, showing off in front of Lady Wonderwhiskers.

But the fan didn't budge. **HOW MORTIFYING!**

"Step aside, Superstilton," scoffed Swiftpaws. "What's needed here is superstrength! And your muscles are less than super."

Then he tried yanking the fan out. *Nothing* happened. So much for superstrength!

"Can I try?" asked Lady Wonderwhiskers.

"Of course," I said. "But be careful!"

"Yes, we don't

want you to get hurt," Swiftpaws added.

A second later, the fan fell down with one **little** push from Lady Wonderwhiskers's pawnail! CLANG!

"If pulling doesn't work, try pushing!" she chirped.

There you go!

Wow!

Swiftpaws and I turned *red* with embarrassment.

"Okay, Heromice," Lady Wonderwhiskers said. "Who wants to go first?"

I stared at the dark, **NARROW** air duct and shivered. Did I mention that I'm afraid of *SMALL, DARK* spaces?

"Come on, **SUPERSTILTON**," Swiftpaws said as he waved me ahead. "You go first."

"No, no," I squeaked politely. "After you."

"No, you," he countered.

My Heromouse partner and I were still ARGUING when Lady Wonderwhiskers climbed effortlessly into the tunnel.

"Follow me!" she instructed.

Once again, Swiftpaws and I turned beet **RED**. We followed Lady Wonderwhiskers into the dark tunnel. A few moments later, we heard a strange *BUZZING* sound.

"Oh no!" Lady Wonderwhiskers cried. "Someone turned on the AIR CONDITIONER!"

"That's okay," Swiftpaws said. "It *is* very hot outside—"

He was interrupted by a blast of cold air.

Whooooooooooooooooooooshhhhh!

Wait, did I say **cold**? I meant **FRIGID**! Within seconds, icicles had formed on our whiskers!

Being a gentlemouse, I opened my mouth

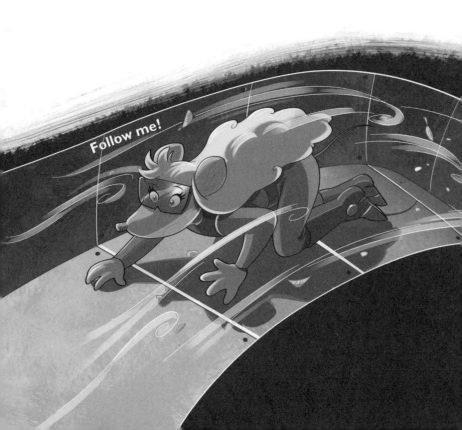

Follow me!

to offer Lady Wonderwhiskers my cape so she could use it to keep **WARM**. But I was so cold the only thing I could say was:

"BRRR! BRRR! BRR! BRRR! BRRR! BRR!"

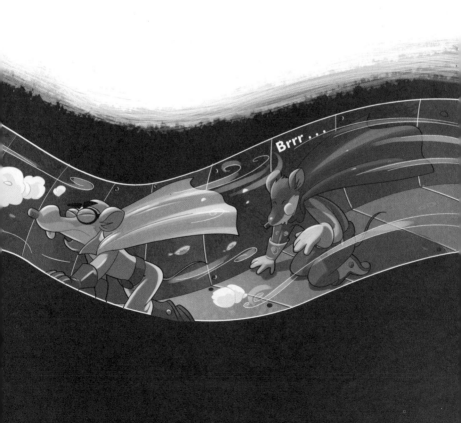

Brrr . . .

A . . . A . . .
A . . . Choo!

When we finally got to the end of that **FROZEN** tunnel, we discovered we were inside the Muskrat TV building's surveillance room. The walls were covered with *screens* showing videos taken by security cameras in different sections of the building. Two **snoring** rodents sat in front of the screens. *Super Swiss slices!* It was **Two** and **THREE**, two of Tony Sludge's henchmice!

But where was **One**?

There was no time to lose. We had to get to the **HUGE** antenna on the roof as quickly as possible. And now we had to make sure we were as **QUIET** as possible, too.

I held my breath as I tried to move noiselessly past the two rats. But suddenly, my nose began to **TWITCH**, my eyes began to **TEAR**, and I let out a loud **sneeze**.

"A . . . a . . . a . . . choo!"

Then I tripped on a wastebasket and bumped into a desk.

Two and **THREE** woke up with a start.

"Huh?!" Two squeaked.

"How did you get in?" Three demanded.

"If we tell you, will you let us go?" I asked **HOPEFULLY**.

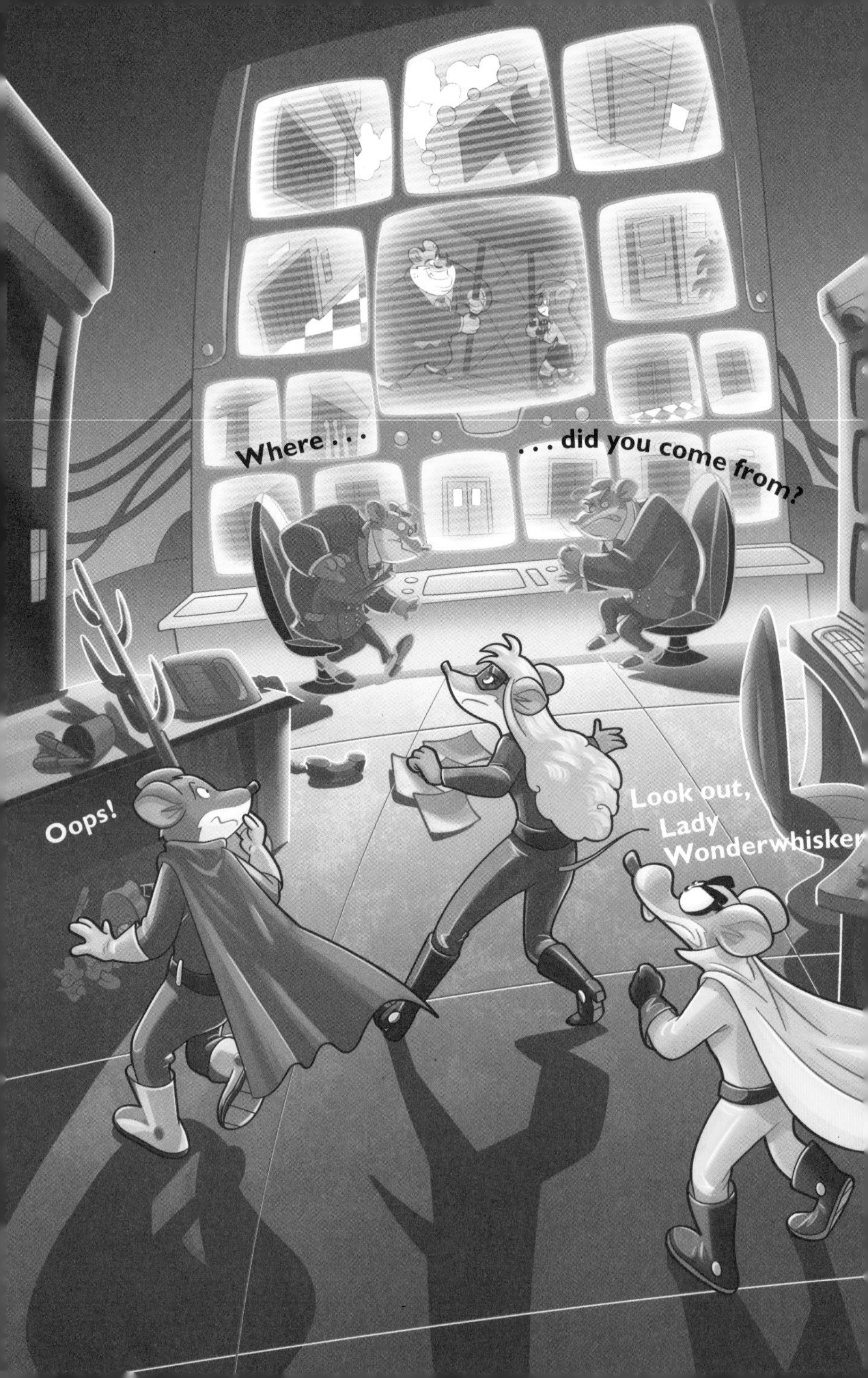
Where . . .
. . . did you come from?
Oops!
Look out,
Lady
Wonderwhisker

As an answer, Two leaped at me. I avoided him by a whisker. Then he turned his attack on Lady Wonderwhiskers. She stuck out her foot and **tripped** him. He landed inside a closet, and I quickly slammed the door and locked it.

Then Swiftpaws shouted, "Supersuit, **BALL MODE**!"

Instantly, my hero partner changed into a large **yellow** rubber ball. With a **bounce**, Swiftpaws ran over Three, knocking him into the recycling bin.

Lady Wonderwhiskers quickly ushered him into the closet, locking the rat inside along with Two.

Swiftpaws changed out of ball mode and back into his normal self.

"*Super Swiss slices!*" he exclaimed. "These rotten sewer crooks have nothing on

us Heromice! They'll be running *scared* the next time we see them!"

I hoped my hero partner was right. We still had to find the **DREADFUL**, dangerous, and downright disturbing Tony Sludge . . .

WE'RE DOOMED!

A minute later, we were **ZOOMING** up in the elevator to the roof.

"We Heromice aren't afraid of anything!" Swiftpaws kept boasting. Then suddenly, the elevator came to a *screeching* halt. Everything went dark.

"Help!" screeched Swiftpaws. "The fuse blew!"

"We're **doomed**!" I cried, jumping into my hero partner's paws.

"I can see you Heromice aren't afraid of anything," Lady Wonderwhiskers said with a chuckle.

I was so embarrassed, I turned as **RED** as a supertomato. At least no one could

see me. That is, until the emergency lights **blinked** on.

Oh, how humiliating!

But I soon forgot all about my **RED** fur. That's because the elevator suddenly began *swinging* dangerously. My fur **STOOD** on end. Did I mention I'm afraid of the dark, heights, cramped elevators, and the librarian at the New Mouse City Public Library? Why is she always shushing me?

Anyway, where was I? Oh, yes, I was stuck in an elevator, **CHEWING** my whiskers to keep from **sobbing**. After all, I didn't want to look like a complete **fool** in front of Lady Wonderwhiskers.

As I chewed, Swiftpaws and Lady Wonderwhiskers **forced** open the trapdoor on the elevator's ceiling.

GREAT GRAVITY! Above us, Slickfur was in the process of **CUTTING** the cables that held the elevator!

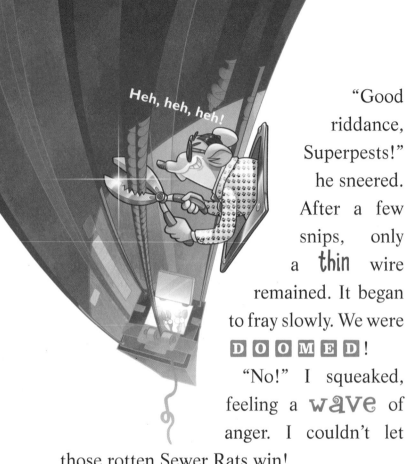

Heh, heh, heh!

"Good riddance, Superpests!" he sneered. After a few snips, only a **thin** wire remained. It began to fray slowly. We were D O O M E D!

"No!" I squeaked, feeling a wave of anger. I couldn't let those rotten Sewer Rats win!

With determination, I grabbed my friends by their paws and took flight as the elevator **DROPPED** away from us. Yes, I, Superstilton, the most superscared Heromouse ever . . . was flying!

I zipped up the elevator shaft.

"Superstilton, you're awesome!" said Lady Wonderwhiskers.

I turned **RED** again, but this time it was for a happy reason.

"*Heromice to the rescue!*" I yelled.

WHAT OILY FUR!

We landed on the top floor and looked around. A *long* corridor led to a room filled with rows of mirrors, racks of clothing, accessories, makeup, and wigs. A dozen EERIE mouse mannequins stood at attention throughout the room.

"This must be the MAKEUP and wardrobe room," said Lady Wonderwhiskers.

"You got that right," echoed Swiftpaws, staring at one of the mannequins. "Look at the WIG on this rat."

We got close to a mannequin with a curly blond WIG.

"What a SOUR expression on this one's snout," Lady Wonderwhiskers observed.

"And what oily fur," added Swiftpaws as he reached out to touch it.

Just then, the mannequin **SPRANG** to life.

"Aw, what do you know!" it shouted.

"It's Slickfur!" I squeaked.

The Sewer Rat replied by **SPRAYING** a cloud of rose powder in our direction. The pink dust covered Swiftpaws and me instantly.

"I can't see a thing!" Swiftpaws cried.

"**ACHOO!**" I sneezed.

Luckily, Lady Wonderwhiskers managed to avoid the ⊏⌶⌷⌷⌸ of powder. With one **acrobatic** leap, she grabbed Slickfur and tied him up.

Serves you right!

Humph!

Once we were sure Slickfur wasn't going anywhere, we **carefully** opened the **STEEL** door that led to the roof.

Tony and Elena Sludge stood in front of us. They had attached the umbrella **rain-triggers** to the large Muskrat TV antenna.

"This TV antenna is going to help us create the flood of the century!" sneered Tony Sludge. "Muskrat City will finally understand that we're the supreme rats around here!"

"You mean the supremely RIDICULOUS rats!" interrupted Swiftpaws.

You're finished, Tony!

Here we come!

Freeze, Rats!

The leader of the Sewer Rats whirled around. "You again?" he exclaimed in surprise.

Meanwhile, Elena *stretched* out a paw to activate one of the rain-triggering umbrellas. Great Gouda, someone had to stop her! But before I could move, Lady Wonderwhiskers leaped through the air and landed next to Elena. Then, with one swift kick, the Heromouse sent the umbrella *flying*. What grace, what PRECISION, what courage!

Elena took off into the building with Lady Wonderwhiskers right on her tail. Swiftpaws and I turned to see the evil Tony Sludge barreling toward us. Good gravity! I wished I felt as **courageous** as Lady Wonderwhiskers. Or, even better, I wished Lady Wonderwhiskers was there to protect us!

As he ran, Tony began **flinging** all kinds of heavy objects at us. These included a toolbox with a complete set of **screwdrivers**, a gigantic potted tree, and a METAL shovel.

"**HEH! HEH! HEH!**" he roared. "You can't stop me!"

HEROMICE NEVER GIVE UP!

Super Swiss slices! Is this how it would all end? Headlines FLASHED before my eyes: *Heromice No Match for Heavy Metal! Sludge Scores Fatal Blow with Set of Screwdrivers!*

But then my hero partner came to the rescue. In a flash, he used his superpowers to change into a gigantic YELLOW shield.

"Take that, Sewer Sludge!" he shouted as I ducked behind the shield for cover. "Heromice never give up!"

Suddenly, disaster struck. That's when Tony threw a long, snaking cable wire at us. The cable wrapped around my paw. I tried to **SHAKE** it off, but instead, I slid right into Tony!

"Great work, Superstilton!" cheered Swiftpaws, grinning from ear to ear.

At first, I had no idea what my hero partner was **squeaking** about. But then I

realized I had **crashed** into Tony just before he activated his flood-making device! Of course, it had all been an accident, but no one else needed to know that, right?

Unfortunately, there was no time to enjoy my little VICTORY.

Don't move!

Gulp!

Heh, heh, heh!

"Give it up, Helplessmice!" a voice suddenly shouted. "Otherwise, your superfriend will come to a SUPER-SCARY end!"

It was the EViL Slickfur. He had Lady Wonderwhiskers!

Lady Wonderwhiskers nodded at Slickfur.

"Elena untied him!" she explained.

Elena had freed Two and THREE next, who were on us like cream cheese on a cracker a second later! We were DOOMED!

LAST WISH

Tony pressed the button on the rain-triggering device. With a menacing **buzz**, the enormouse antenna started to work.

"Now we'll start a **storm** that will never be forgotten!" cackled the Sewer Rat. "Especially because it'll be the last one you'll ever see! Heh, heh, heh! Get ready for a nice **bath**, Superpests!"

The gigantic antenna dish continued buzzing *louder* and *louder*.

A flash of **lightning** shot toward the sky, and a moment later, the strongest storm I had ever seen burst from the sky! A **TORRENTIAL RAIN** poured down on us and **soaked** us from the tips of our whiskers to the ends of our tails. The

rats got ready to go back to the sewers of Rottington.

"What do we do with the **PRISONERS**, boss?" Two asked Tony.

"Do I have to tell you everything?" Tony hollered over the sound of the rain. "Tie them to the antenna! The **STORM** will take care of them!"

What a tragedy! What a disaster! What a **COSMIC CATASTROPHE**!

I had to do something. But what? Suddenly, I came up with a **brilliant** idea.

"Wait!" I squeaked, turning toward Elena. "You wouldn't get rid of us without granting us one **last wish**, would you?"

She looked at me with a curious expression. I could tell she was dying to know what my last wish would be.

"Well, okay, that seems reasonable," she said. "What would you like?"

"I would like to chew GUM!" I answered. "I have a couple of sticks in my belt."

Swiftpaws understood immediately what I had in mind.

"Oh, yes!" he added, eyes SHINING. "Superstilton must have one last piece of GUM!"

"That's your last request?" Tony snorted. "I always thought you were fools, but now I know for a fact—you're superfools! Elena, untie this Helplessmouse so he can get his ridiculous GUM and we can get out of here!"

Elena quickly untied my paws while Two

watched over me. I took the superinflatable rafts Tess had given us out of my belt and let them fall into the water pooled around my ankles.

PLOP! When they hit the water, the micro-rafts inflated until they had changed into **YELLOW** super-rafts! I took a deep breath and sprang into action. I jumped into the first raft and, keeping my **balance** like a surfer, slid toward Two and Three, knocking them down. Then I headed toward Tony and Slickfur. They, too, went snoutfirst into the water.

"**Rats!** I just cleaned this suit!" Tony shouted when he hit the water.

I ran to free Lady Wonderwhiskers, and she **rushed** to turn off the rain-making superantenna. Just like that, the storm stopped, and the sun began to **SHINE** again on Muskrat City. Finally, I untied Swiftpaws.

"Listen!" he **SQUEAKED**.

We heard a police siren in the distance.

"You're going back to jail, Sludge!" chuckled Swiftpaws.

"We'll see about that!" sneered **One**. He had suddenly appeared, and he was flying Tony's helicopter . . .

Oops!

I had forgotten about **One**!

Before we could do anything, Tony, Elena, and Slickfur **JUMPED** into the helicopter, and Two and Three grabbed

the helicopter's skids. A second later, the helicopter lifted into the sky, carrying the Sewer Rats 𝒻𝒶𝓇 away from us!

You Are Whiskerful!

In the end, the **sewer rats** escaped, but at least we had saved Muskrat City.

When we got back to **HEROMICE HEADQUARTERS**, there was a huge celebration in our honor! Tess prepared a whisker-licking-good lunch that included three **gooey** cheese pies, freshly squeezed lemonade, a carrot cheesecake with cheddar frosting, and huge slices of **juicy** watermelon.

Swiftpaws and Proton began stuffing their snouts immediately. But I still had some unfinished business to take care of.

I wanted to tell Lady Wonderwhiskers how much I admired her **STRENGTH**

and **courage**, and now seemed like the perfect time. Oh, if only I wasn't such a **nervous wreck** when it came to speaking my mind to **smart**, beautiful female rodents.

My heart was **beating** out of my fur as I turned to Lady Wonderwhiskers. "Ahem, Whiskers, I mean, Lady Wonder, um, that is, I, well, I wanted to say that you are whiskerful, I mean . . ."

I was about to finally get to the **POINT** (well, okay, maybe it would have taken a little longer, but I was getting there) when something hit me on the ear.

SNAP!

OUCH!

I turned to discover I was being **pelted** with watermelon seeds.

"That's a **bull's-eye**!" Swiftpaws

exclaimed as he passed a slice of watermelon to Proton. "Here, you try."

I was FUMING.

"Lady Wonderwhiskers and I were in the middle of a very *INTERESTING* conversation, and you interrupted us!" I complained.

"Really?" teased Swiftpaws. "Well, it couldn't have been that *INTERESTING*, or she wouldn't have left."

I turned around. Lady Wonderwhiskers was no longer sitting next to me. Instead, she was squeaking with Tess and Electron. A few minutes later, she thanked us for our help, **waved** good-bye to everyone, and left. *RATS!*

I *hung* my head. If only I had had the courage to tell Lady Wonderwhiskers how I really felt about her. Now the moment was

gone. Dejected, I turned to Swiftpaws.

"Cheer up, **SUPERSTILTON**!" he said. "Want a slice of **watermelon**? It's fabumouse!"

Suddenly, I realized there was a better way to cheer myself up. I would go on my

Cheer up, Superstilton!

Sigh!

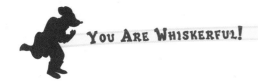

VACATION! Who doesn't love a vacation?

"No, thanks," I said, feeling a bit better. "If I hurry, I can get to **Whiskers by the Water** in time for my *SQUEAKA SQUEAKA* lesson on the beach!"

I said good-bye to the gang at Heromice Headquarters. Everyone **HUGGED** me, then waved.

"Come back to visit us soon, Superstilton!" they called.

On Cape Cheddar Beach

I wish I could say I soared **gracefully** into the clouds, but I didn't. I still hadn't gotten the HANG of taking off, so Swiftpaws had to help me. Basically, he

Cape Cheddar, here I come!!

used his superpowers to pick me up and *PROPEL* me into the sky! GOOD GRAVITY!

After a while, I started to relax about the whole flying thing. I mean, don't get me wrong—I was still afraid to look down. But the wind **WHIPPING** through my whiskers felt nice, and the sun warmed my fur.

I reached the beaches of Cape Cheddar just as the sun was setting. It was so *BEAUTIFUL*, I hovered over the sand, entranced. Unfortunately, right then, my Heromouse costume vanished, and I **TUMBLED** to the ground.

I **hit** the beach with a loud smack, bounced on my tail, and smashed into a palm tree. Then before I could even shake off the sand, something pinched my tail.

Ooooouch!

"Ouch!"
I jumped so **HiGH**, I could have won an Olympic gold medal. (Well, okay, maybe I couldn't have actually *won* a medal, but you get the point.) An extra-crabby-looking crab glared at me, then SCUTTLED away in a huff.

Despite my **throbbing** tail, I was happy. After all, I was on vacation!

I listened to the waves gently lapping the shore. Then I dipped my pawnail in the water. Ah, still nice and **warm** from the day, just the way I like it. I decided to take a quick snooze before dinner. How could I resist the softest bed on the coast? But just as I started to stretch out on the sand, I heard a loud sound.

Kaboom!

I looked around, trying to figure out where the noise had come from.

Then it hit me. No! It couldn't be! But I knew deep down that I was hearing the unmistakable sound of thunder! Rotten cheese rinds!

In just a couple of seconds, the sky darkened, and a light drizzle began to fall. I sighed. There wasn't a thing I could do, and this time, it wasn't even Tony Sludge's fault!

I ran for cover at a place called The Flying Fur Café. I sat down in a comfy chair facing the ocean. Even with the rain, the view was spectacular.

I sipped a scrumptious mozzarella MILKSHAKE while I watched the rain fall. If I was going to get stuck in a RainstoRm, I was glad I was at this mouserific beach resort. Plus, it

was only a matter of time before the storm passed and the sun came out.

And if there was one thing I had learned that week, it's that a **HEROMOUSE** never gives up, even when he's faced with a sudden downpour. That's because nothing is **impossible** for the Heromice!

DON'T MISS ANY HEROMICE BOOKS!

#1 Mice to the Rescue!

#2 Robot Attack

#3 Flood Mission

#4 The Perilous Plants

#5 The Invisible Thief

Be sure to read all my fabumouse adventures!

#1 Lost Treasure of the Emerald Eye

#2 The Curse of the Cheese Pyramid

#3 Cat and Mouse in a Haunted House

#4 I'm Too Fond of My Fur!

#5 Four Mice Deep in the Jungle

#6 Paws Off, Cheddarface!

#7 Red Pizzas for a Blue Count

#8 Attack of the Bandit Cats

#9 A Fabumouse Vacation for Geronimo

#10 All Because of a Cup of Coffee

#11 It's Halloween, You 'Fraidy Mouse!

#12 Merry Christmas, Geronimo!

#13 The Phantom of the Subway

#14 The Temple of the Ruby of Fire

#15 The Mona Mousa Code

#16 A Cheese-Colored Camper

#17 Watch Your Whiskers, Stilton!

#18 Shipwreck on the Pirate Islands

#19 My Name Is Stilton, Geronimo Stilton

#20 Surf's Up, Geronimo!

#21 The Wild, Wild West

#22 The Secret of Cacklefur Castle

A Christmas Tale

#23 Valentine's Day Disaster

#24 Field Trip to Niagara Falls

#25 The Search for Sunken Treasure

#26 The Mummy with No Name

#27 The Christmas Toy Factory

#28 Wedding Crasher

#29 Down and Out Down Under

#30 The Mouse Island Marathon

#31 The Mysterious Cheese Thief

Christmas Catastrophe

#32 Valley of the Giant Skeletons

#33 Geronimo and the Gold Medal Mystery

#34 Geronimo Stilton, Secret Agent

#35 A Very Merry Christmas

#36 Geronimo's Valentine

#37 The Race Across America

#38 A Fabumouse School Adventure

#39 Singing Sensation

#40 The Karate Mouse

#41 Mighty Mount Kilimanjaro

#42 The Peculiar Pumpkin Thief

#43 I'm Not a Supermouse!

#44 The Giant Diamond Robbery

#45 Save the White Whale!

#46 The Haunted Castle

#47 Run for the Hills, Geronimo!

#48 The Mystery in Venice

#49 The Way of the Samurai

#50 This Hotel Is Haunted!

#51 The Enormouse Pearl Heist

#52 Mouse in Space!

#53 Rumble in the Jungle

#54 Get into Gear, Stilton!

#55 The Golden Statue Plot

#56 Flight of the Red Bandit

The Hunt for the Golden Book

#57 The Stinky Cheese Vacation

#58 The Super Chef Contest

#59 Welcome to Moldy Manor

The Hunt for the Curious Cheese

#60 The Treasure of Easter Island

#61 Mouse House Hunter

#62 Mouse Overboard!

Don't miss my journeys through time!